Theresa's Journey

The Green Star Lake Series

Robert Checkwitch

Published by Green Star Lake Books

ISBN: 978-0-9730475-3-0

Cover photography by Craig Popoff, Canora, SK Cover image: Janelle Straightnose

Contact: rciezk@yahoo.ca
Printed in Canada

Theresa's Journey
The Green Star Lake Series

Contents

CHAPTER 1

Winnipeg

Theresa looked out the window of the 10-seater airplane as it circled over Winnipeg before landing. It was the first time she had been this far from Green Star Lake. Her year-old son, Chance, was on her mind for most of the trip. She had never been away from Chance for more than a couple of days, but now she realized she wouldn't see her son until Christmas. The thought depressed and scared her, even though she knew her mother would take good care of Chance. She hoped that his father, Jimmy, her former boyfriend, would spend more time with him so he could get to know his son.

As the plane hit the runway her first thought was to get off the plane, get her things then buy a ticket back home. It would be easy. Then she wouldn't have to deal with all the unknowns that twirled in her head. Everybody got off the plane, leaving her as the only remaining passenger.

The pilot turned around and looked at Theresa with a questioning expression. Finally, after a couple of minutes he asked, "Are you getting off?" and then smiled at her. "Do you need help?"

"No, no," she blurted out, "I'm fine, just fine. I don't need help."

She forced herself to get up and made her way to the front of the plane. The pilot stood beside the door waiting patiently.

"I think everything is going to be fine," he said.

What did he know about her life and what she was facing?

It was Theresa's first time in Winnipeg, and at seventeen she was hoping to complete her high school and go on to a nursing program.

She made her way out of the cabin onto the stairs leading to the asphalt, then headed for the small terminal used for northern flights. When Beatrice, her Cree counsellor in Winnipeg, saw Theresa she waved, approached and put out her hand.

"Theresa, I'm so glad to meet you. How was your flight?"

"Okay," Theresa replied. She was glad to see her counsellor. She had spoken to her on the phone only a few times from Green Star Lake.

"Well, come on, let's get your luggage, then we can go."

Theresa was anxious to get out of the crowd of people at the airport. She went with Beatrice to the pile of luggage, picked out her own, then followed Beatrice out to a blue van.

They headed out of the airport. Theresa was stunned when she saw the size of the buildings, the hundreds of cars and the crowds of people everywhere. She had been to Thompson, but it was nothing like this. Everybody seemed to be in a hurry, driving, walking, talking.

Beatrice pulled the van into a restaurant parking lot. "I thought you might be hungry after your flight."

"Not really," Theresa answered.

"Come on. I'm hungry, and this will give us some time to talk about things."

They sat in a booth and ordered.

While they were waiting for their food, Beatrice asked Theresa what she knew about Winnipeg and whether she had any friends in the city.

"No."

"Well that's okay, you'll get to know it. You're going to a very good high school, and I've arranged for you to live in a very nice part of the city. It's one of the best areas in Winnipeg. At the high school you're not going to see many First Nations students. There's probably about forty in the school, mostly from the north and some from Winnipeg."

"How big is the school?" Theresa asked.

"Around eleven hundred students in grades 10 to 12."

Theresa tried to imagine what a school with 1,100 students would be like. The whole community of Green Star Lake had only 1600 people, and the school had just 285 students from kindergarten to grade 10. That would mean that you could fit most of the people from the community into one building. How could that be possible?

Beatrice knew what Theresa was thinking. "It's a very big building with 25 to 30 students in each class."

Theresa tried to imagine that. Her grade 10 class had only 11 students. It sounded scary to her, 30 students and not a person she knew. She was starting to feel lonely and isolated.

Beatrice could sense this. "Hey, you're not going to be bothered at the school. You'll see, they're going to be friendly. I'm taking you to the school tomorrow, so you can meet some people before you start on Monday. One small step at a time."

Theresa thought about one small step. What was Beatrice thinking? These weren't small steps, they were giant leaps—the plane ride, a strange city, meeting her counsellor who was asking all these questions, going to a new school with all new students. Theresa didn't see it as a step but as a giant leap.

Beatrice was reassuring. "The first few days are the hardest, Theresa, but everybody who comes in from the north faces this. Don't be too quick to get scared and start jumping to conclusions. Give it a chance, go slowly, let it sink in gradually.

I'll be here to help you."

"Help?" Theresa asked.

"Yes, if you have trouble at school or where you're living, anything."

Theresa didn't want help right then; she just wanted to be by herself in a room where she could close the door.

"Open your eyes to the possibilities, Theresa. Don't shut them from fear of the unknown. There's a lot of opportunities for you out there, so try not to pass them up."

All Theresa could think about was home, just to be able to sit in her bedroom, talk to her mother, her friends, Chance and Jimmy.

But Beatrice wouldn't let up. She had been here many times before with new students from the north, knowing they were feeling the fear, the instant loneliness and the thoughts of home.

"I'm not sure I…" Theresa started.

"Theresa, I was you 25 years ago. I got off that plane feeling exactly the same way you do right now. I know what you're going through. Believe me, I understand."

That made Theresa feel better. She looked at Beatrice in a different way now. Some small connection had been made.

"Are you willing to give it a good try?"

She thought about all the people in Green Star Lake who were hoping she would succeed. She thought about what Chance would think years later if she gave up and what it would be like to face Jimmy if she didn't try. She quickly made up her mind.

"Yes, I'm ready," Theresa told Beatrice.

"Good. I'll be honest with you, Theresa. Many students from the north come, many make it and some don't. I'll talk about the reasons in the next few days."

But Theresa didn't want to wait for a few days to know why some students didn't make it. She wanted to know now.

"Why do students fail?" she demanded.

"We don't need to talk about it now, Theresa. We've got lots of time."

"I would like to know now."

Beatrice was surprised at Theresa's assertiveness but was pleased. A good sign, she thought, a mind of her own in that pretty head.

"They got dragged into a world that they had never experienced before. There's lots of temptation out there, Theresa, lots of freedom to make mistakes."

"What do you mean, lots of freedom?"

"You come from a small community where not much goes on, right?"

Theresa nodded.

"Everybody knows you back home; you had lots of friends. Sure there were some bad things going on. There is in every community, but you didn't want to let your mom down…right?"

Theresa agreed. It was true.

"You're going to be on your own most of the time, so even though you're going to be staying with a good family, they're not going to force you to study or not to stay out all night with new friends. They'll take care of you, but they're not going to be your mom and dad."

She thought about her dad. She hoped he was still in Winnipeg so they could spend time together.

"All I'm telling you is that with the freedom comes a lot of temptation, risk and the need for self-discipline. Do you know what I'm talking about?"

Theresa knew. Just last year one of the students from Green Star Lake had come back home after two months in Thompson. She came back and got into drugs as a way of coping with the failure, yet Theresa knew that two had gone on to university.

"Yeah, of course."

"So now you've got to find the toughness and self- discipline to get through the next few years and finish grade 12. I'll be here to get you through the tough times, but mostly it has to come from you."

Without her mom, friends, Chance and even Jimmy, Theresa really wondered if she could cope with the emptiness that gripped her. She didn't say a word, but from the look in her eyes Beatrice knew she understood.

Beatrice pulled up to her new home. "This is Norm and Susan's house. You're the fourth student they've boarded in the last eight years. They're nice; they don't do it for the money. You can tell by the house that they're pretty well off. Two of the students graduated from high school, and the last one stayed for five months, went back home, came back a couple of times and is still trying to get her grade 11 finished. She's living some place else but still visits now and then." Beatrice talked about the student as if something had gone wrong. Maybe it was the tone of her voice or the way she looked off to one side.

"When was the last time she was here?"

"About six months ago."

As they got out and started to unload Theresa's belongings, Norm and Susan came down to meet them. Beatrice introduced Theresa. Susan gave her a hug, but Norm didn't look at her directly. Instead, he held back, standing off to one side, as if he were judging her. The couple took Theresa into the house and showed her the bedroom. It was large and modern with warm wood furniture.

Then they all sat down in the living room and talked for about a half hour. Theresa said very little but tried to be polite, answering their questions about her home in Green Star Lake. Finally, Beatrice got up. "I'll pick you up around noon tomorrow. I want to take you over to the school before classes start."

Theresa nodded. She was unhappy that her only connection in Winnipeg was leaving. Norm and Susan continued to ask her a lot of questions, and Theresa tried to tell them as much as possible about Green Star Lake, but she was tired and finally excused herself. She was planning to unpack her things but lay on the bed and was asleep in a few minutes.

The next morning Susan had a big breakfast on the table. Theresa wasn't hungry, but that didn't stop Susan from putting food in front of her.

"I guess you're a little nervous, eh?"

Theresa nodded. She wasn't sure what to make of Susan. She found her very talkative and curious, asking a lot of questions. She felt uncomfortable, as if she were being interrogated, although she knew that Susan was not being rude. She sensed that Susan wanted to know more, so she could understand what Theresa was all about. It was different, and Theresa knew that she would have to get used to it quickly. You didn't ask people too many questions in Green Star Lake, especially if you didn't know them. Now that she was surrounded by white people, she accepted that she would have to get used to a different culture and different attitudes.

Theresa looked around the kitchen. Much of it was stainless steel—the stove, the fridge, the oven, and part of the counter top. The cupboards were made out of beautifully grained wood and the floor of square stones streaked with green and black. Everything looked incredibly modern, as if it were just out of the store, everything, even the pots and pans. Theresa didn't know whether to be impressed or turned off by it all. All of it put together gave her a cold distant feeling, even the shining sparkling wood. She was almost afraid to touch anything.

"Do you like our kitchen?"

Theresa paused. "Yes...it's...very modern."

"We like it that way. We put it all in last year."

Theresa didn't say anything.

"Beatrice should be here pretty soon. Is there anything else you want?"

"No…I'm fine."

"Well, you just have to ask, any time. We want you to be comfortable and feel at home."

Theresa thought it would be a while before she could feel comfortable in this house. For one thing there were no smells of wood burning, moose meat cooking, bannock or blueberry pie

baking. It was as if she were in a sealed container, thoroughly clean but without a sense of reality.

She went back to her room. It felt good. She lay on the bed for a while, studying everything. Norm and Susan had done a good job of fixing it up—nice wood furniture, warm colors on the walls and ceilings, and a large bed. In the back of her mind she knew that she could come to like this place, and the thought made her feel nervous. It could make going back to Green Star Lake difficult. A small warning in the back of her brain told her not to get too comfortable, not to start liking her new home too much, because some day she would have to leave it. She sensed that she would have to discipline herself against being drawn into this lifestyle and wondered whether this was the kind of temptation Beatrice was talking about.

Theresa was waiting for Beatrice outside when she pulled up.

"Well, how was your first day?"

"Okay."

"Just okay?"

"It's very nice."

"And how did you get along with Susan and Norm?"

"We just talked for a while, but I was pretty tired. I'm not sure about Norm though. He seemed kind of distant. Does he really want to do this?"

"He takes a little getting used to, Theresa. It will be okay, and I bet you were tired. All the changes are a little overwhelming at first. Is your dad in Green Star Lake? I heard a rumor that he was in Winnipeg."

"Yes, he's in the city somewhere. I haven't heard from him for a couple of months."

"Do you want me to see if I can locate him?"

Theresa thought about that. Did she want Beatrice looking for her father? But these thoughts were overcome by the worry about him. She had written to him in the last four months, but had not received a phone call or a letter in a long time. She had been more upset about it than she was willing to admit to herself or anyone.

"Yeah, that would be good, Beatrice." She could see that Beatrice wanted to help her.

"Okay, I'll see what I can do over the next few weeks but no promises."

Theresa didn't want to talk about it any more.

They walked into the high school. When they got through the front doors she saw halls of classrooms going in four directions. She could barely see the ends of the halls. The school was huge. Theresa began to feel uncomfortable when she realized that in three days she would be in the middle of an enormous group of students. It was hard to imagine how they could fit 1,100 students into this one building.

"It's big, very big," she said to Beatrice.

"Yes, but it can be very interesting and lots of fun. Let's go see your counsellor."

"I thought you were my counsellor."

"Outside of school, not in school. That's going to be Janet. She's great. She's been the counsellor for students from the north for the last 10 years. You'll like her. Everyone gets along with her and likes her. She can really be a help if you get into difficulty at school."

At the counselling office, Beatrice introduced her to Janet, who was not what Theresa had expected. Janet was older, at least 60, or maybe more. How could she talk to her? Even her mother was younger than this lady, but then she thought about one of the Elders at home, a wise woman who always seemed to be able to help people. Maybe this white woman also had special abilities, so Theresa decided it was too early to judge her. Janet gave her a big smile.

"I'm going to leave you now, Theresa," Beatrice told her. "I'll be back in about an hour after you and Janet have talked about your grade eleven timetable and books."

Janet caught her look. "Hey Theresa, what can you tell me about yourself?"

Theresa had never been asked that question before, and it seemed all she ever did after landing in Winnipeg was answer questions. "I'm from Green Star Lake." She stopped.

"Yes, I know that." Janet waited.

"What do you want to know?"

"Well, about you, about your family, your community, school, anything."

"I passed grade 10, I live with my mother, and my father is somewhere here in the city."

"Do you have brothers, sisters, anybody else in your family?"

Theresa thought about Chance, but was reluctant to tell Janet, who knew about the baby but wasn't going to push it.

She waited.

"Yeah, I've got a son." She realized quickly that Janet would have known this from the school information that probably had been sent from Green Star Lake.

"Ahhhhhhhh, wonderful, how old?"

"Just about a year and a half."

Janet saw a beautiful smile break out on Theresa's face, and she could see the tears start to come in her eyes.

"My mom is taking care of him right now and sometimes his father."

"Father?"

"Yeah, Jimmy." She lowered her head. "We're sort of partners."

"Sort of?" Janet looked at her.

"Yeah, sort of." Theresa smiled.

Janet didn't want to pursue that. It was much too early. She wanted to say something to lighten the situation. "Well, we never know with men, do we?"

They both laughed.

"So it must be really hard to be away from Chance?"

Theresa stared at the ground for a while, then the tears began to roll down her cheeks. She couldn't speak.

Janet took her hand and squeezed it. "I hope you've got a big picture of him on your wall."

"Just a little one."

"We have a very modern computer lab in the school, so if you can bring a photo we can blow it up. It won't cost you anything."

"Okay, I'd really like that." Then she pulled a small photo of Chance from her wallet.

"That's a good looking little boy, Theresa."

Theresa flashed a big smile. "He's..." her voice trembled, and she stopped as she tried not to cry.

"Why don't we talk about something else, Theresa. You'll probably be seeing him before too long."

After discussing Theresa's possible course choices, they decided on history, art, and math.

"I'm not too good at math, so maybe I should leave it to the last term."

"Yes, I can see from your grade ten reports that all your marks are good except math, so why don't we get you a tutor? I have a grade twelve student who is excellent in math and gets along well with everyone. He's offered to do some tutoring this year. I think the two of you would work well together."

Theresa thought about it. "I guess Jimmy was my tutor back home. He was good at math."

"But you probably helped him in language arts, right?"

"Jimmy never asked for help from anybody, even when it could have made things easier for him. He always wanted to take care of himself."

"Jimmy sounds like quite the guy. What's he doing now?"

"He's back at school. At least that's where he's supposed to be. The last time I talked to my mother she said that he had gone back."

"What grade?"

"Ten. He's trying to finish it."

Janet wondered how old Jimmy was but decided to leave it until later.

"I think I'm going to need help. Where do we do the tutoring?"

"In the library, at lunch, before or after school, or on the weekends, there are lots of options. Volunteer tutoring looks good on their applications for university."

Before Theresa knew it an hour had gone by. Janet got up and stuck out her hand, but when Theresa went to shake it, Janet took both of her hands, squeezed them, and then took her on a tour of the school.

"You're going to do just fine. I've met a lot of kids from the north, and they do pretty well." Theresa wondered what Janet meant by pretty well.

Beatrice and Theresa spent the rest of the afternoon driving around Winnipeg. They dropped into a few malls where

Beatrice bought Theresa school supplies and other items she would need.

When they got back home, Beatrice told her, "You're just in time for supper; they'll be waiting for you. How would you say your day was?"

"I think pretty good. Janet is nice."

"Yes, she can really help you if you have problems. But you have to let her know. She'll go out of her way to make things work for you."

Theresa thought she'd have to get used to all the people who were helping her. It seemed important to them that she be successful. It was as if they were counting on her.

"I'll see you Monday morning. I'll pick you up around eight for your first day of school."

"I think I'd rather take the bus on the first day, you know, with everybody else."

"Great, then I'll phone you Monday evening to see how things went."

CHAPTER 2

First Day

Monday morning Theresa was up two hours before her alarm went off. She was nervous. She decided that the sooner she got into the routine and stopped worrying about what was going to happen at school, the better off she would be. Susan told her where to catch the bus and offered to walk with her to the bus stop on her first day, but Theresa didn't want to feel like a kindergarten kid. When she got on the bus she saw it was filled with young people, most of whom got off at the school.

Inside the school, she was stunned by the crowds of students in the main hall. She was used to a mix of little kids and older students, but as she stood in the middle of the hall she was surrounded only by teenagers. When she arrived at her first history class in room 209, she found only one other student in the room. She took a seat at the back, got out her books and within a few minutes her history teacher entered the room. He was an older man whose appearance and behavior seemed quite disorganized. He got some papers out of his briefcase, then some books, shuffled them around on his desk and made an attempt to organize everything in small piles.

The rest of the class poured in within the next few minutes.

It was a double period class with a 10 minute break. She listened, didn't ask any questions, sat at her desk through the break and left with an assignment for the next day. Her history teacher may have been disorganized, but she enjoyed his enthusiasm.

Nobody talked to her, although several students had smiled at her. It turned out to be a pretty ordinary day. At noon she ate her lunch outside on the grass at the side of the school. Even though it was a beautiful day in Winnipeg, Theresa's thoughts wandered back to Green Star Lake and what everybody might be doing. She decided that her first day at school had been less overwhelming than she had expected.

Janet had asked her to come to the counselling office at the end of her last class When she arrived, Janet was standing there with a boy who was slouched against the wall. He was tall, slim, with a full head of curly red hair that fell over his forehead. He glanced out the corner of his eyes, as he tried to look at her without making direct eye contact.

"I'd like you to meet Bruce, Theresa."

Bruce didn't look up.

"Hello, Bruce."

He still didn't look up but did a small wave with his hand.

"Bruce, you can do better than that. Come on, you're in grade 12."

"Hi." He still didn't look at Theresa.

"Bruce has offered to help you with math." Janet looked at Theresa as if she expected her to say something.

Theresa didn't know what to say because Bruce appeared very uncomfortable and uninterested. Theresa waited.

"This is your first time tutoring, isn't it, Bruce?" Janet asked.

He gave a quick nod and stared at the ceiling.

Theresa was feeling uneasy.

"I'd like the two of you to spend a few minutes together to discuss how you'd like to do this."

"Now?" Bruce spluttered.

"Well, you're both here aren't you?" She waited for an answer. "Theresa?"

Theresa said nothing. She could tell Janet was getting irritated with Bruce.

"Well?" said Janet and stared at Bruce. There was a long period of silence.

Finally, Theresa suggested, "Maybe we could go outside."

"Good idea," Janet told them.

Theresa opened the door and walked out, figuring that if he came, fine, and if he didn't that was fine also, because Janet would get her another tutor. When she looked back, Theresa saw Bruce talking excitedly, waving his hands in the air. Finally he stomped through the door and followed her outside.

Theresa walked to the middle of the yard in front of the school and sat down on the grass, but Bruce told her he wanted to go behind the school.

"Okay."

"Yeah," he said, tromping around the far end of the school and sitting down on the grass away from the entrances.

"How does this work?" Theresa asked.

"What?"

"Tutoring."

"Haven't done it before, why?"

"I just want to know what we do."

"I teach you. That's not too hard to figure out is it?" He seemed angry.

"You sure you want to do this, Bruce?"

"Yeah, why're you asking?"

"You don't look too happy about it."

"I'll do it."

"You don't have to tutor me if you don't really want to." Theresa felt as if she were dealing with a stubborn ten-year-old.

"Janet will get another tutor for me."

"I said I'd do it."

"So where do we start?"

He lay back on the grass but didn't answer.

Theresa figured it was best just to leave him. She was getting tired of this.

"You're an Indian, aren't you?"

She just looked at him.

"Never talked to an Indian before. Didn't know they were so good-looking."

Theresa got up to leave, but Bruce stood in front of her blocking her way.

"That wasn't an insult, it's just that I've never talked to an Indian girl before."

"So now I think I understand."

"What?"

"You were mad with Janet because she wanted you to tutor me? Maybe you should go back to see if she can get you someone who meets your expectations."

Bruce avoided her eyes.

"I think you should get someone else to tutor."

"What do you mean?

"A girl like you were expecting… right?"

Bruce stared at the ground. He hadn't expected her to be so forceful.

"That's why we're at the back of the school so no one would see you with me. Is that right?"

"You're angry."

"And you're a coward." Theresa was mad now. She didn't get angry often, but when she did it was hard for her to control herself. She left him sitting on the grass and headed for the bus stop.

"Hey Theresa, wait for me." She didn't turn around. When

she arrived at the bus stop, she realized that he had been following her.

"I'm sorry. Can we meet again tomorrow?"

"Where, out by the garbage cans?"

"No, I'll meet you right there beside that tree."

As the bus pulled up, she didn't answer him, but as she got on and sat down she had a good feeling. Perhaps she could handle this new life.

After school the next day, Theresa was walking toward the bus stop when she heard someone calling her name. It was Bruce. He was sitting in the middle of the grass in front of the school waving at her. Theresa stared at him, unsure of what to do.

"C'mon, I've been waiting for you."

Theresa slowly made her way to where he was seated but remained standing, glaring at him.

"Did you bring your math book?"

"Are you sure you want to do this, Bruce?"

He stared at the ground. "You were right about yesterday; I was expecting someone else. I made a mistake. Can we start again?"

"What, here?" she asked.

"It's a nice day, and we could walk down to the park or stay right here in front of the whole world."

Theresa knew what he was talking about and realized that he had been stung by her remarks about his not wanting to be seen with her.

"Let's go back to the library," she suggested.

When they sat down, he began to question her about what she knew in math. He asked her many questions which she could not answer. As the questions continued, they got easier until Theresa was able to answer a few of them.

"What grade did you finish before you came down here?"

Bruce asked.

"Why?" She was getting irritated.

"Well..." but he didn't finish.

"What, tell me."

Theresa could see that he didn't want to answer. "I know I'm not good at math. I've always had trouble, but I passed grade 10."

"And how are you finding the math here?"

"It's only the second day.... but pretty hard."

"Yes, I can understand that. Look, Theresa, some of the questions I asked you are from about grade 9."

She knew she was behind, but this shook her. "What do you mean grade 9? I passed grade 10."

"You wanted to know, so it's better if you have a good idea of how much we need to cover."

"Do you want to quit?"

He smiled when he looked at her. "No, of course not. I don't want to quit. What do you take me for?"

Now Theresa could see that he was irritated. She smiled at him and he smiled back. Theresa could tell there was a lot more in his smile than she had expected. She sensed a twinge of longing in his look but couldn't understand why she thought that. She just felt it, as she had so many times before with people, like an unspoken message, some kind of telepathy.

"We'll start from where you're at. It's the only way. How much time have you got?"

"A couple of hours. I have to be back at my place around 6:00."

As he worked his way through the math problems that Theresa was able to handle, the hour passed quickly. Gradually he moved forward with slightly more difficult problems, but when she struggled he gave her advice and made suggestions without actually doing the work for her. Sometimes when she looked up he was staring at her, smiling.

He offered to drive her home, but she wasn't ready for that for some reason.

She was standing at the bus stop when he went by in his car, waving at her. Theresa asked herself why she had insisted on taking the bus.

CHAPTER 3

Back at School

Back in Green Star Lake, Jimmy was now two weeks into the school year and was uncomfortable with being in school with kids so much younger than he was. He had heard about upgrading for older students, but it wasn't available in Green Star Lake. Louise Quintel, last year's teacher, had been replaced by a young, first-year teacher. He was unhappy that she hadn't come back to the community. He missed her. The principal had changed also, an older guy with grey hair who seemed okay but was a little too strict for Jimmy. The last guy was pretty flexible, didn't judge people too quickly and had even let him back into school after juvenile detention without a lot of questions and rules. So he had a pretty good year, even though he missed a lot of school again.

Jimmy wanted to pass grade 10 so he could graduate in the spring and then join Theresa in Winnipeg, where he could finish high school. He wondered if he could hang in for one whole year straight.

He tried to spend time with Chance, his son, but he didn't know what to do after an hour or so, and usually ended up taking him back to Theresa's mother, who could give him all the love and attention that Jimmy was still not able to offer. At times Jimmy's grandmother would spend time with Chance. She loved being with him.

Every day he wondered what was happening with Theresa. He had been expecting a phone call from her, but it still hadn't come. He visited Theresa's mother, who told him that Theresa had phoned a couple of times and was doing well. She was happy with where she was staying, and school was going well for her. Theresa's mother explained that a grade 12 boy was helping her with math, the way Jimmy used to do.

"It's making a big difference," she told him.

When he left Theresa's place, Jimmy had only one thing on his mind, another man in Theresa's life. What was this about? When he thought of this special tutor, Jimmy's imagination began to spin many pictures. Jealousy and anger rose in his chest even though he knew he had no right to feel jealous. He had never been too kind to Theresa, but he remembered the last time he had seen her at the airport before she left and still heard her words, "I'll see you at Christmas." He saw it as a promise, a commitment, but what did Jimmy know about commitment?

He told himself that he had no right to be angry and no reason to try to control her life, but his heart would not pay attention to his head. He tried hard not to think about it, but it ate away at him day and night.

Finally, Jimmy went into the bush for the weekend and got high on gas and alcohol with his friends. When he got back home his grandmother wouldn't look at him as he came through the door. It took him until Thursday to get back to school. He walked into his math class, but after five minutes put down his head and fell asleep. Jimmy stayed for the first class and then walked to the airport to find out what it would cost for a ticket to Thompson. He still had $250 from working in the summer. He knew he could hitchhike the 540 kilometres from Thompson to Winnipeg.

Lying in bed the next morning, he tried to figure out what to tell his grandmother.

"I'm going to Winnipeg."

His grandmother was sitting at the kitchen table drinking tea. She didn't say a word. She got up and gave him a big hug. "Stay out of trouble, Jimmy." As he was walking out the door she put $50 in his hand.

"No, I can't take this. I've got money."

"Yes, take it, Jimmy. It will help, and say hello to Theresa."

He turned to look at his grandmother and knew from the look in her eyes that she understood why he was going.

As the plane took off for Thompson, Jimmy looked back at the community. He wondered when he would be coming back and what waited for him in the city.

After hitching rides for three days and sleeping in abandoned cars, he finally arrived in Winnipeg. That night he slept in a park. When he got up the next morning he could feel the change in the air as he watched the clouds move rapidly across the sky.

He knew the name of Theresa's school, so it was easy to get directions from people. After trying to figure out the bus system he decided to walk. Two hours later he arrived at the school, just as it started to drizzle. He felt dirty, tired and hungry.

Jimmy walked into the main hall across from the administration office. Large groups of students moved past him as he stood with his hands in his pockets, staring down the halls wondering what to do next. Many were so well dressed—jackets with logos, sport shirts, tight tank tops. Others wore the usual jeans and T-shirts or the super baggy athletic shorts with oversize baseball caps. Some of the girls wore short skirts.

It was like a fashion show.

A few students stopped to look at Jimmy as he stood in the middle of the hall with a lost look in his eyes. He couldn't help looking the girls up and down; it was a natural response to their obvious good looks and the way they walked, laughed and smiled. A few of the younger boys giggled when they saw him.

Jimmy began to feel foolish, stuck in the hall in his dirty jeans, smeared t-shirt and old gym shoes. He hung his thumbs in the pockets of his jeans, trying to decide his next move when a cute young blonde approached him, gave him a big smile and stopped a few feet in front of him.

"You look lost." She wasn't looking at his face but eyeing him up and down.

Jimmy had always known he was good-looking. Plenty of girls had told him that and had tried to hook up with him from the time he was teenager, but this was different, a good looking blond girl. He was surprised at his mixed feelings. He felt stupid standing there, searching for something to say.

"Yeah, I'm looking for someone."

A group of students walked up behind the girl and suggested she come with them.

"Looking for someone?"

"Yeah."

One of the guys in the group, a well built, athletic type, spoke. "I think you're in the wrong part of town. Head to the north end and you'll find all your friends there."

"He said he was looking for someone in the school," the blonde replied. "Back off, Mark."

Jimmy started to feel the muscles in his arms tighten. It was a warning. He knew it. He always felt it before a fight and told himself to walk away but instead blurted out to Mark, "I wasn't talking to you."

Mark moved forward a few steps toward him. "This isn't an Indian reserve. You look like you belong back in the bush."

Jimmy's fist started to come back, but before he could do anything, the girl stepped between them.

"Mark, get out of here. Come on, let's go to the office. My name is Laura." She took Jimmy by the arm and led him to the office. "Who are you looking for?"

Jimmy told her and she spoke to the secretary.

"Theresa is in history class right now."

"So what's your name?"

Jimmy hesitated.

"Is it a secret?" She leaned closer to him.

He laughed. "Jimmy."

"You're going to have to check in with the office, everybody does, but it's no big deal."

Jimmy hesitated. He'd always avoided authority, but he knew he had no choice.

In the office, the vice-principal went to the intercom to ask Theresa to come to the office. "She'll be down in a few minutes; she's just about finished her class."

Jimmy wandered back out to the main hall where Laura was talking to Mark.

Theresa gave him a big smile when she saw him. "Jimmy, what are you doing here?"

Jimmy didn't answer but had a good feeling wash over him. Theresa noticed that he looked pretty ragged with his dirty jeans, scruffy T-shirt and a scar that was healing on his cheek, but even with his unshaven face and tough, sinewy, arms poking out of his dirty shirt, he still looked handsome.

"Lets go outside," she suggested.

As they were walking toward the entrance they heard Mark ask, "Is this place turning into a bloody reserve?"

Theresa turned around to see who had made the comment,

so she didn't see Jimmy quickly move behind her and grab Mark by the front of his shirt, viciously jamming him against the wall. Before Theresa could move, Jimmy had grabbed Mark by the throat and was rearing back with his right fist, ready to slam it into Mark's face.

"Jimmy," Theresa said softly, "Jimmy, don't."

Fist clenched, he held Mark against the wall for a couple of seconds. Theresa had seen that look before, the hot, violent anger in his eyes, a sign that he was ready to battle anyone into submission and take the consequences.

He hesitated for a second. Theresa touched him on the shoulder. Then he turned to look at her. Mark's face was turning red. Jimmy let him go and sauntered slowly through the doors. He never looked back at the crowd of students gathered at the entrance. He didn't stop when he got outside, even though Theresa was trying to catch up to him.

"You okay?" she asked. "Come on, let's go over there."

She pointed to a bench at the far end of the school yard. She finally got him to sit down, but she could tell from the tension in his body and the look in his eyes that he was still furious. She put her arms around him, gave him a squeeze and talked softly to him while he cooled down.

They saw Laura coming across the grass toward them. She introduced herself to Theresa. "The vice-principal wants to see us in the office."

Jimmy immediately got up and walked away. Theresa called to him to come back, but she knew that there was no chance that he'd go back to the school.

"It wasn't his fault; Mark was hassling him," Laura told her. "I guess he'll have to get used to it if he comes to the city."

The vice-principal told them he was more interested in talking to Jimmy than to them. Mark was standing in the office with a rebellious look on this face.

"Well, what have you got to say, Mark?" the vice-principal asked.

Mark shrugged. They all waited.

"Okay, I made a couple of comments, not enough to get that guy going nuts."

"Too bad Jimmy's not here so you could apologize, but on the other hand, Theresa, we can't have your friends brawling in the school, especially since he's not a student here."

Theresa nodded, but she was furious at Mark, not Jimmy, and now she began thinking it might have been a good idea if she had let Jimmy pound him.

"If he's coming back tell him I want to see him. I'm not mad at him, but I want to talk to him if he's in the school."

CHAPTER 4

New Friends

Jimmy headed downtown. He had no idea where Theresa lived, and with so much happening he had forgotten to ask her. That night he again slept in a park under some bushes, and when he woke up the next morning it was much colder. He could tell from the smell in the air, the look of the sky, and the colors of the trees and bushes that it was going to be a cold week. He wondered what to do next.

He thought about walking back to the school, but decided against it. He was beginning to feel small because he was out of his environment, small because everybody at the school looked so cool and rich, small because he was lost in the city where he knew no one. Who was he but some First Nations guy barging in on all those successful white students and embarrassing Theresa? He began to think that it might have been a mistake to come to Winnipeg with only a little money and no friends. Even Theresa didn't seem happy to see him. Feeling lost was new for him. Even in juvenile detention he had always thought he was in control, as if he could handle anything that came his way, no matter how tough it might be or how big the guys were who challenged him. He never backed down, but here in the city he didn't know who he was fighting against. As he looked at the tops of the huge office buildings and hundreds of cars speeding past, the city made him feel unimportant. As he walked north along Main Street the buildings became older. Some were in good condition, but within a few blocks things changed, and now he began to see empty places and an old hotel, with people just hanging around outside.

After he crossed under the Main Street railway tracks, and had stopped to look in the window of a pawn shop, he was approached by three young First Nations men. When they came up behind him the oldest put a hand on Jimmy's shoulder and started to pull him around. Jimmy resisted but one of the others yanked on his shirt spinning him around. "Who're you, asshole?"

Jimmy didn't answer. He prepared himself for what might come next.

"I'm asking one more time," said the biggest guy, moving face-to-face with Jimmy. Jimmy could smell the alcohol on his breath.

Jimmy was pushed back slowly.

"You think you're tough do you?"

"Tough enough."

"Where you from, kid?"

"Green Star Lake."

"No shit. I had a girlfriend from Green Star. What're you doing in the city?"

"Here to see somebody."

The oldest and toughest of the three stepped back and gave him a hard look while Jimmy prepared for what might come next, but a grin broke out on the guy's face as he put out his hand. Jimmy took it with relief, and the two connected.

"Welcome to the city. This is our territory. I'm Nick, this is Alex and Garth." He took a long look at Jimmy's body as well as the look in his eyes, quickly deciding he would make a good gang recruit. Nick put his arm around Jimmy's shoulders. "Want to come to a party tomorrow night?"

Theresa hardly slept that night after the surprise of seeing Jimmy at the school and the fight in the hall. She worried about why he had come to the city, where he was staying and what had happened at school in Green Star Lake. Had he quit school? It was a worry she didn't need.

She left for school early, so she could work on her math before seeing Bruce that afternoon. She kept looking for Jimmy in case he came back to the school, but nothing happened.

After tutoring, Bruce asked if she would like to get something to eat. She couldn't refuse him after all the time and effort he had put in. As they pulled out of the parking lot in Bruce's car, Theresa saw Jimmy across the street, leaning against a telephone pole with his arms crossed. Her first instinct was to tell Bruce to stop the car, but she was afraid of another fight. Theresa didn't look back, but as they drove away she felt embarrassed and ashamed of herself. She told Bruce to turn around, but by then Jimmy was gone.

"What was that about?" he asked.

"Nothing. We can go now."

Over a pizza, Bruce talked while Theresa listened. Theresa had come to understand that it was going to be like that when Bruce wasn't tutoring. He talked about his car, his father, his friends, his sisters and his lack of success with girls. At first Theresa couldn't figure out why Bruce would have trouble getting a girlfriend. He was good-looking and smart. Then she realized that he lacked confidence.

"You're nice to be around," he said, looking at her with affection.

Theresa was uncomfortable. "That's nice, because we spend a lot of time together; it would be hard if we didn't get along."

"How would you like to go to a movie on Saturday?"

"I don't know. A friend is in Winnipeg but maybe some other time."

"Yeah, we all heard about your friend from the north. Kinda violent isn't he?"

"That wasn't his fault."

"Well he'd better be careful if he comes around the school and challenges the white or Asian guys."

"He didn't challenge anyone. Mark insulted both of us."

"You'd better get used to it because I'm telling you for your own good."

"Is that how you think, Bruce?"

He could tell she was getting angry and decided to drop the subject.

Theresa was anxious to leave as soon as they finished eating. When they got to her house Bruce tried to talk to her.

"I'm sorry about your friend, Theresa…" but she was out of the car as he called after her, "I'll see you on Thursday."

He was puzzled about why she was so mad. He'd only told her for her own good, the way anybody at the school might have done, but still somewhere in the back of his mind he sensed that he had done something wrong. He often felt that way.

Jimmy remembered the conversation he had with Nick about the party.

"You'll meet a lot of people and some good-looking girls."

"Yeah, for sure, I'll be there," Jimmy had told him.

Nick asked, "You got a phone number where we can get hold of you?"

"No."

His new friends had taken him out to eat, but when he was ready to leave Nick reminded him, "See you tomorrow. It's going to be a great party, lots of good stuff."

"Definitely, Nick, I'm coming, no way I'd miss it."

Jimmy called Theresa's school and persuaded the school secretary to call Theresa to the office by pretending that he was Theresa's brother, phoning with an emergency from Green Star Lake.

When she got on the phone, he didn't mention what had happened at the school the day before or ask how she was doing. "I met some guys who are having a party tomorrow and I'd like you to come."

"Who are these people, Jimmy?"

"They're some guys I'd like to get to know. I think it could be good."

"Why, Jimmy? How long are you planning on staying in Winnipeg?"

He avoided the question. "Will you come with me or not?"

She knew she had to go because she had no reason not to, and besides, she wanted to spend time with him, find out about Chance, his new friends and if he was actually back in school.

"Okay," she answered, but she was not happy. It sounded suspicious, but then things often did with Jimmy.

When they got to the party the next evening, the place was packed. Theresa could tell right away that this was a rough group of people, from teenagers to people in their thirties. Theresa had a bad feeling about it. She wanted to leave after a few minutes, but Jimmy disappeared with a couple of his new friends toward the back of the house. Someone offered her a beer, and she decided to accept it because she needed something to relax. She looked at the other girls who were dressed in jeans, tight tops or skimpy, revealing blouses. Theresa had overdressed and felt out of place. She needed the beer to get over her nervousness.

An hour passed, but Jimmy had not returned. Several young

men approached her, asking questions, complimenting her on her looks and making suggestive comments. Some of the men were nice—they seemed intelligent and funny, but others were rude. While on her second beer, she started to relax and began talking to some of the women. They asked who she was with or was she just 'available'. When she told them about Jimmy, they gave her a blank stare.

Finally, Jimmy returned for a few minutes but left again before she had a chance to tell him that she wanted to leave.

As the time passed several people began pairing off. Because it made Theresa uncomfortable to watch, she got up to look for Jimmy. She took her beer and headed upstairs to the second floor, but began to feel dizzy as she reached the top. She saw three bedrooms with closed doors and went to open the first even though a warning in the back of her head told her it was not a good idea, but the beer was pushing her forward. In the first room two couples were lying on the floor. In the second there were only a couple of young guys, who invited her to stay. When she turned to leave, the biggest one quickly closed the door and blocked her way.

They joked with her as Theresa tried to get to the door, but she was yanked back onto the bed before she could move. The two of them pushed her onto her back and held her down. She started to scream, but a large, smelly hand pressed down over her mouth.

"You think you're such a classy bitch, hey? We're going to take you down a few steps."

She was struggling and kicking as they tried to pull off her pants. She began to cry. Then the door opened and a husky, young First Nations man came forward. "What's going on here, Tony?"

"What do you think is going on, Keith? Just close the door and you can join in the fun."

When Keith saw the fear in Theresa's eyes, he pointed at the big one. "Let her go."

The two men hesitated but when he made a move toward them, they loosened their grip on her and moved off the bed.

Keith stared at them. "Out! Get the hell out!"

The two men scrambled through the door. Keith sat down beside her.

"It's okay. Everything is going to be okay now. You don't have to worry. Nobody's going to hurt you."

She stopped crying and sat up on the bed.

"What's your name?" he asked.

"Theresa. Thank you."

"I think we should get you out of here, Theresa. What do you think? Did you come by yourself?"

"No, I came with my friend Jimmy. Do you know him?"

"Sorry, I don't. Do you want a ride home? What do you want to do?"

"Jimmy, I want to find him."

"Okay, let's go look."

They found Jimmy with three other guys sitting outside on the grass. Theresa saw the faraway, glazed look in his eyes that she had seen many times before at Green Star Lake before he went to juvie. "Are you ready to go, Jimmy?"

He didn't answer, couldn't answer even though he tried. "Go…where…now...I don't think…"

But Theresa saw he was gone on drugs and wasn't coming back for quite a while.

Keith drove her home. She learned he was a university student and was also from the north, a community about 100 miles from Green Star Lake. As they pulled up to the house she thanked him again. "You've been very nice."

"You're nice, too, maybe too nice to be hanging out with that crowd. They're pretty good guys when they're sober but can be a little nasty when they get into whatever they're taking."

He asked for her phone number.

"I might call you to check up on how you're doing." He touched her hand. "Be careful."

Theresa was very glad to be back in her room.

CHAPTER 5

In the Gang

The first month of school passed quickly. Theresa had not seen or heard from Jimmy since the party. She was disappointed and disgusted that he had not protected her that evening. Theresa began to think that it might be better if they didn't have contact for a while. Even though she worried about him, she knew he wasn't telling the truth about his trip to Winnipeg, and now he was hanging out with a very tough gang. She could worry about him only so much if he refused to be honest with her. Besides, she didn't want him hanging around the school or where she lived. You never knew what he was going to do next, because he never talked about what he was thinking and had a way of being evasive, interested only in what he wanted and not the consequences. Theresa had lived with the uncertainty and conflict from the first day she had made love with him, always getting pulled back and forth from love to despair. She didn't think she could take it any longer. Was he ever going to change? Not likely. She could see him being easily drawn into the gang life, the easy money and excitement.

When she met Bruce on Thursday for tutoring, she found him quiet and distant. He avoided talking about Jimmy or anything to do with First Nations and white people. When they finished he got up.

"See you next Tuesday," he said and started to walk away, but Theresa caught up with him and asked, "Are you okay, Bruce? You're not mad, are you?"

"Naw, what would I be mad about, Theresa?"

Theresa could tell something was bothering him. "Come on, Bruce, what's bugging you? Tell me."

He said nothing.

"Okay, Bruce, I'll see you next Tuesday." She walked away, but he called after her, "Theresa…"

By the time she turned around he had decided to keep going in the opposite direction without finishing what he had started to say.

Theresa thought it was hard to figure out some of these white people in the south. You never knew what they were going to do next.

Jimmy didn't sober up for two days. His first thought when his head was clear was about Theresa. Where had she gone? He remembered little except arriving at the party and getting into some meth and whiskey. He'd slept in the basement, not recalling what had gone on the previous few nights except that he'd met a lot of people. It turned out it was Nick's house, where he and six of his friends stayed. When Jimmy came up from the basement Nick and nine other guys were sitting around the kitchen. Nick told him to sit down, and Jimmy quickly figured out they were planning their gang activities for the next couple of days. He listened to them for four hours. He heard some discussion, some arguments but mostly orders from Nick about what was to take place.

When everybody was leaving, a guy asked him, "Didn't you come with that good-looking young thing a couple of days ago?'

"You mean Theresa?"

"She's got a helluva a body, Jimmy," laughed Tony, recalling the scene in the bedroom with her.

Jimmy tensed and clenched his fists, but Nick was quick to cool things off. "Let's quit with this bullshit and start doing what I want." He came over to Jimmy and asked him to stay, but Tony couldn't resist a parting shot. "Anyway, Keith took her home and I'm sure he's a happy man," smirked Tony.

"You got a place to stay?" Nick asked.

But Jimmy wasn't interested in where he'd be staying. "Did you see what happened to my girlfriend that night?"

Nick saw it as an opening to influence and control Jimmy. "I can find out, but it sounds like she went with Keith."

"Keith, who's Keith?"

"Don't be worrying. I'll find out what happened." But Nick knew exactly what had happened. He had watched Keith walking Theresa out to his car. Nick knew that Theresa had been in the bedroom, and he had been thinking he'd like to have Theresa for himself.

"Don't worry about what happened. I'm sure everything is okay. When are you bringing her back?"

"Dunno, why?"

Nick ignored the question. "I've got a job for you if you want to make a few bucks."

"What?"

"Just take this small package downtown, give it to someone and get an envelope from him."

"What's in the package, Nick?"

"You don't need to know. It's not important?"

Jimmy knew it had to be drugs, but Nick was right when he said he didn't need to know, because he was out of money, something Nick knew and used to his advantage.

"Do I get anything?" Jimmy asked.

"Fifty."

"What do I have to do?'

"Here's the address of an office building downtown. You'll meet a guy standing right next to the entrance of the underground parking garage across the street, and you'll give the package to him, then he'll give you the envelope. Simple as that."

That sounded simple to Jimmy. "Sure, why not?"

"Okay, this afternoon at 4:30. I'll meet you back here at 6."

Jimmy nodded and left with the package. Nick thought about warning him not to take off with the drugs or money but didn't think it was necessary. Besides, Jimmy would know he couldn't stay in Winnipeg if he took the money; he would be a man on the run if he tried to rip Nick off. Nick was feeling satisfied because Jimmy would be a good young man to train. Jimmy had that fearless look in his eye that told Nick he wouldn't cave under pressure. Fearless, without friends and money, Jimmy made the perfect gang recruit.

Jimmy spotted the man leaning against the wall of the parking garage at 4:30. As he approached him, he turned and walked slowly into the darkness of the underground garage. After the man grabbed the package from Jimmy, he handed over an envelope and walked slowly away, farther into the lines of parked cars. It was over in a matter of seconds. He then started walking back to Nick's, to get the $50 he needed. It occurred to him later how easy it might have been for that guy to be the police. The thought didn't stay with him for long, though, because he was thinking about Theresa and a guy named Keith. He wanted to find out what had happened that night at Nick's place.

CHAPTER 6

Keith

Keith phoned Wednesday, just after Theresa had hung up the phone following a fierce argument with Jimmy about her going home with another guy. She ended up slamming down the phone, and the phone call from Keith made her feel a lot better. When he asked her to go out the next night, the argument with Jimmy faded.

The next day Keith picked her up in front of the school, and they drove to a restaurant. Theresa enjoyed being with him, his easy way of talking and the positive attitude he had towards his classes at university and his life in general, but what she liked the most was the interest he took in her life, her baby, and Green Star Lake. It made her feel good, having someone ask about her without thinking they were only asking for information.

"That was quite a night you had at the party. How did you get yourself into that?"

"Stupidity, beer, not knowing anyone except Jimmy."

"Ahhhhh, Jimmy, tell me about him."

"He's struggling right now. He missed nearly all of last year, so he just started school again, cause he's trying to get his grade 10, but he really hates it. Now he's here in Winnipeg for some reason he hasn't explained to me."

"How long is he staying?"

"I don't know. We had a very bad argument last night about those new friends he's making, and he asked about you."

Keith steered the conversation in another direction. "How's school?"

"It's pretty good other than math, but I've got a tutor; art and history are going really well. I'm enjoying both of them. The art class is great because I'm working on a project with symbols and materials from up north."

"That's sounds great. I'd like to see it when you're finished, Theresa."

"Sure, but it won't be ready for about a month. It's a big project, about 30 per cent of our final mark and in history I've got one of the top marks in the room."

Before Theresa realized it, two hours had passed while she sat in the booth looking at Keith, talking and listening to him talk quietly about the north and home. She thought about the things she could learn from Keith. This was a lot better than dealing with Jimmy.

They agreed to go out again. "I'll call you on Friday, Theresa."

Back in her bedroom Theresa's thoughts about Keith pushed Jimmy to the back of her mind.

Beatrice continued to call Theresa to see how she was doing. At first, every three or four days, but as school and her life continued to improve, their conversations became shorter, although Theresa knew that she could call Beatrice whenever she needed. Beatrice dropped into the school to see Janet, Theresa's school counsellor.

"She's doing very well," Janet said. "I'm impressed with her attitude and willingness to work."

The next time Beatrice saw Theresa she told her, "You're off to a good start, Theresa. Keep it up."

They talked about many things, but Theresa didn't tell her

about Keith, the party and Jimmy's coming to Winnipeg. She didn't want Beatrice to start worrying and there was no reason she had to know. "Have you found out about my dad yet?"

"Sorry, not yet, but I haven't given up."

"I wonder where he is."

"It might take a little while, but I'll find out what's going on. He might have left the city which would make it hard to find him."

"Doesn't anybody know where he is?"

"I talked to a fellow who saw him about a month ago at one of the hotels."

Most of the time Theresa shut out any thoughts of her father, because she was afraid that thinking about him might bring bad news. When Beatrice dropped her off at home she gave Theresa a hug.

"Keep it up, you're off to a great start."

When Keith arrived at the house on Friday, Theresa introduced him to Susan and Norm. They were surprised that Theresa had met someone so quickly.

Although she was only 17, Keith took her to a bar, where they listened to music with some of his friends. They were different from the people she had met at Nick's party. She enjoyed the conversations with them. After leaving the bar they went back to Keith's and watched a movie. Theresa had been reluctant at first to go back to his place, but Keith convinced her that she had nothing to worry about. After the movie, he took her home, walked her to the door, and kissed her. Later, Theresa thought about the fun time she had with Keith, not like the many times she'd fought with Jimmy. Keith was different, thoughtful, kind and understanding. Perhaps going to the party with Jimmy had not been a waste of time, because she had met Keith. She could hardly wait for the next time she would see him. That night she had a happy dream about her and Keith on the lake back home.

CHAPTER 7

The Lesson

Two weeks passed. Jimmy had decided that it was best not to contact Theresa. Why did he need her when he had met other girls since hooking up with Nick? Let her wait. Besides, he was too busy since becoming a drug-runner for the gang. Each day brought new activities—stealing cars, breaking into buildings, and collecting from people who owed Nick money, which sometimes required physical violence. Then there was the fight with a rival gang after a night of drinking at one of the hotels. It was a brutal brawl. One of the guys from the gang got stabbed in the shoulder, but Jimmy held his own. He enjoyed the fight with equals, but beating up defenseless people who owed Nick money bothered and embarrassed him. He realized it was necessary, but it depressed him and made him feel small. There was no challenge in being a bully.

His favorite activity was stealing cars with an experienced member of the gang. The two of them managed to grab three cars in two weeks and delivered them to a barn in the country. The money was good; his life was exciting; lots of girls were available; and drugs and liquor were always close at hand when the anger and frustration about Theresa ate at him. The fact that she was going with Keith, whom he had seen only briefly, made the anger boil inside, but his pride prevented him from phoning her. Shutting her out of his life was the only way he could go on. Jimmy had never shown that he needed her and never would. Why would he need her now, when he had money and several girls who wanted him?

It was two in the morning when he got back to Nick's after the fight. Instead of going into the house, he lay on the grass. It was one of the last warm fall days. As he stared at the stars the dream came. He was walking with his grandmother along the lake, holding her hand, listening to her beautiful, soft voice. She stopped and pointed across the lake as the sun began to burn off the early-morning fog. In the distance he saw his best friend, Gary, who had committed suicide last spring, canoeing across the water. Within a few seconds a strong wind whipped up the waves. Gary paddled furiously against the wind and the waves and then stopped, turned, raised his hand and pointed at Jimmy as the canoe slowly slipped below the water. When Jimmy turned around, his grandmother kissed him on the cheek and hugged him tightly, laying her silvery head on his chest. He held her and turned back to look for his lost friend. He stared at the lake, which had become calm and was shimmering with sunlight, but when he turned to take his grandmother's hand, her image gradually faded from his sight and then returned as she walked toward the lake. In his dream, he tried hard to focus on the small figure of his grandmother. At the edge of the trees he saw Theresa looking at him, not moving, not saying anything, just staring at him.

Jimmy bolted upright from the ground in a cold sweat. This vision disturbed him as did many he had had since childhood, because he was unsure of its meaning. He had learned that there was little he could do to stop the dreams and had come to accept that they were gifts, something to be appreciated, but he wasn't feeling that way in the middle of the night as he wiped the sweat off his forehead. As he lay back on the grass, a quick succession of pictures flashed through his head—sitting with his son Chance on the dock back home, lying with Theresa in the grass making love, arguing with his mother, whom he had seen only twice in the last year, racing across the ice with his best friend Gary on their machines, frying fish on an island out in the lake with his father, who had been shot in a hunting accident, and taking down a caribou with his uncle on one of their hunting trips. The images were so clear that Jimmy thought he could put his hand through an imaginary window and touch them.

He was still sleeping outside when Nick woke him the next morning. "We got a problem, and I want you to get going."

Jimmy was still half asleep. "What, what time is it?"

"Never mind, get your ass off the ground and let's get your shit in gear."

"Yeah, yeah." Jimmy would have preferred to go back to bed in the house, because he wasn't ready to start taking orders so early in the morning. He was feeling weary and heavy in his chest. "I don't know, Nick. I'm pretty tired after the fight last night."

"You get your ass up to the house," Nick yelled at him. "Two of the guys are waiting for you."

Nick gave them the address of a house in the west end of the city. "You go in there, beat the door down if you have to, and you tell that asshole he either pays me today or we're going to beat him to death. He's owed me twenty-five hundred dollars for the last month, and I don't care if his wife and kids are there. Do it in front of them if you have to. Do you understand?"

Nick glared at them. "Don't come back without the cash."

Nobody said a word as the three of them headed for the car. When they stopped at a red light, Jimmy opened the car door and got out.

"Where you going?"

"Two of you is enough to do it. I'll meet you back at the house."

"Nick's going to be really pissed off at you."

"Yeah, yeah." Jimmy walked away.

When he got back to the house later in the afternoon, Nick stopped him at the front door. "What the hell did you think you were doing this morning?"

Jimmy stared him and didn't answer.

"Oh, I see, tough guy, you're not going to answer?"

Jimmy was silent. He had learned that keeping quiet was best when in trouble.

"When I tell you to do something, you do it." He waited for Jimmy to respond.

"Do you need three guys to beat up one skinny runt?"

"That's not the point. The point is you let me down, you did what you wanted, your own thing."

Jimmy didn't need any more of this, but as he tried to get past, Nick grabbed him and shoved him against the wall. Three other guys appeared from the kitchen and began to beat him viciously. When they finished, he was lying on the floor covered in blood.

"Now maybe you'll listen," Nick yelled at him.

When he finally got up a half-hour later and stumbled outside, where Nick and the guys were sitting on the porch drinking, Nick smiled at him. "You got the picture now, Jimmy?"

The other gang members were quiet but not hostile toward him. One of them joked, "You know Jimmy, sometimes we've gotta teach you guys from up north a little lesson. You gotta learn we gotta stick together. It's all we got, buddy."

Jimmy said nothing, grabbed a beer and sat down. One eye was closed, his ribs hurt, and both his lips were swollen, making it difficult to drink.

"Yeah, sometimes we have to break in you young wild stallions," another guy joked.

They all laughed and joked about it, but inside, Jimmy seethed with anger at the idea that anybody could try to control him. The violence of people he considered to be his friends surprised him, but he told himself that he should have known better. Violence was the main tool of gang life, something Jimmy didn't find surprising, but not being in control was new. For the first time in his life he felt a small sense of defeat, as if he was giving into something stronger than himself. He didn't like it. Even being held in juvie hadn't done that to him. He might lose a fight, but he was always in control of his life, but now, sitting on the porch, he saw Theresa and the life he had known slipping away. It scared him.

CHAPTER 8

Bruce

Theresa finally agreed to go to a movie with Bruce, although she told him she could only go on Thursday. She wanted to keep Friday and Saturday open for Keith with whom she had spent the previous two weekends. Theresa and Bruce went to eat after the movie, and Theresa enjoyed the evening, even though she sensed that Bruce was hoping and expecting that she would see him as more than just her math tutor. It was close to midnight when Bruce turned onto a side street and stopped in a shaded area at the end of the block.

"Why are we stopping?" Theresa asked.

"I just wanted to talk to you before I drop you off."

"What about?"

"I'd like to go out with you more often, Theresa."

Theresa noticed the change in Bruce's personality from a confident, comfortable tutor to a talkative, nervous teenager.

"You're a beautiful girl," he said, bending over and trying to kiss her on the cheek as she turned away.

"Bruce, stop it, what are you doing?"

"Please, Theresa; I've wanted to do this for so long." He put his arms around her while she sat as stiff as a log.

“Bruce, stop, now.” But he pulled her close and held her tightly.

“Please, just a little,” he pleaded.

She grabbed his wrist as his hand moved up to her breast. “I just want to be close to you. I really like you, Theresa.”

They began to struggle as Theresa tried hard to push him away, but he kissed her on the neck.

“Bruce, you’re being such an idiot, stop embarrassing yourself.”

He slumped back in the seat, letting her go. “Yeah, okay, but I thought you’d be willing to do it with me; you girls are like that, aren’t you? That’s what I’ve heard.”

“Do it…do it. Bruce…..us girls…what girls…girls like me... desperate girls from the north?” She began to raise her voice. “You think that because you’re helping me with math I’m going to sleep with you? Do you? Do you?”

“Well…I guess not, Theresa.”

She opened the door and began to get out, but he grabbed her arm and wouldn’t let go. “Please Theresa. I’m sorry, please stay in the car…. I’m sorry.”

She relaxed. “Okay, but quit being such a fool. You’re acting like a 12-year-old.”

His was head was slumped down on his chest. “Yeah, that was stupid, but I just want to be close to you. I think about you every night in bed and wish you could be there so I could hug you. You’re right, I’m an idiot.”

Theresa reached out and gave his neck a squeeze. She was feeling sorry for him now, not mad. “Have you ever had a girlfriend, Bruce?”

“Not really, not a real girlfriend.”

“Not really?”

“Last summer I went out with a great-looking girl I liked a lot, but she dumped me after a couple of weeks.”

"Why?"

"I don't know, maybe because I'm a total geek."

"Geek?"

"An awkward social misfit with lots of brains."

"I'm surprised. You're good-looking. You're smart. You like to help people. You don't drink and do drugs. You're nice to people...."

He interrupted her, "Most of the time," and Theresa knew he was referring to what had just happened.

"Do you ever ask girls out now?"

"Sure, a few I really like, but nothing happened....only that one."

They sat and talked for an hour until Theresa finally told him what was on her mind.

"I'm going to give you some advice, Bruce. A lot of girls would be interested in you if you didn't act so desperate, nervous and unsure of yourself around them. Girls like to have fun, talk about themselves, laugh, relax on a date, not feel uncomfortable because you're so uptight." She was thinking about the way Keith made her feel. "Quit trying to take out the hottest girls in the school and go with some of the girls you can have fun with and talk to so you don't feel like such a geek. Take an interest in them, and quit talking about yourself all the time."

He tried to apologize again, but Theresa told him, "You're a nice guy, Bruce; get out there and have some fun and quit hoping to make it with the queens."

He started up the car without saying a word. When they pulled up in front of the house he turned off the car and smiled at her. "Thanks, I'll think about what you told me."

Theresa could see he seemed relieved, and she knew that their relationship had changed; they had become friends. She bent over and kissed him on the cheek. "You can take me out to a movie any time you want Bruce."

"I'll see you at the library on Thursday. You're pretty wise for a young girl."

"We grow up pretty fast in the north, Bruce."

CHAPTER 9

Jimmy's Decision

Monday morning at 11, Theresa was called to the office. The vice-principal was waiting for her. "Your friend is waiting for you out in front of the school." He walked her to the front door, pointing to Jimmy, who was leaning against a car across the street. "If he's planning on coming into the school, I want him to come to the office to see me first."

As Theresa crossed the street Jimmy started to walk away. By the time she caught up to him, they were a block away from the school. "Where are you going, Jimmy?"

"Nowhere." When he turned around she saw the black eyes and cuts on his face.

She ran up to him. "How did you..." but before she could finish, he put his hands up as if he was going to push her away.

"I hear you've got a boyfriend." Theresa was silent.

He yelled at her. "As soon as you get to the city you're getting it from your pretty guy."

Theresa knew he was about to explode with rage.

"If you've come to yell at me, I'm leaving."

"What about us?" he yelled at her.

"What about us? You're hanging out with a gang and look at you. Do you expect me to hang around waiting for you to grow up and quit being a stupid kid?"

Jimmy just stood glaring at her with clenched fists and rigid arms.

"It's true, Jimmy. All you want to do is act tough, fight. and get high. I'm not waiting for you because you'll always be screwed up. It's true and you know it. Chance doesn't need a loser like you in his life so why don't you go back to your creepy gang? You belong with them, not us."

She watched as his whole body relaxed, his shoulders dropped forward and his arms uncoiled. He stopped looking at her. His gaze fell to the sidewalk. Then without a word he left her standing there. Theresa walked back to the school with a heavy heart. She had never seen Jimmy looking so defeated.

Jimmy walked to the centre of the city and sat on a bench in a park. He wished he could get on a bus to someplace far away where nobody knew him. He fell asleep, and when he woke up, he felt soft, cold snowflakes falling against his cheek. He started walking for the highway north to Thompson. It was dark when he stepped onto the shoulder with his thumb in the air, waiting for a ride that would take him towards home. With $20 in his pocket, a thin jacket and an October snow in his face, Jimmy was not looking forward to the trip.

When he finally reached Thompson he was broke. He phoned his uncle from Thompson to ask if he would buy him a plane ticket home.

"Of course, Jimmy. Your grandmother is very sick, so get here soon."

Although his ticket was waiting for him when he got to the airport, he had missed the plane to Green Star Lake by a half hour. Knowing that the next flight would not be until the following afternoon, he found an old abandoned truck, crawled into the cab and tried to fall asleep.

Beatrice had not talked to Theresa for two weeks and was anxious to find out how she was doing. "Everything okay, Theresa?"

"Yes, I think so. I've made some friends at school and I've met a great guy." She told Beatrice about Keith and Jimmy. Her mother had told her that Jimmy had arrived home last week.

"I think it's good that he went back home, for you and for him."

"Yeah, he'd just get into trouble here and make my life difficult."

Beatrice wondered about Keith, whom Theresa kept talking about. It concerned her. "How much time do you spend with him?"

Theresa knew from the way Beatrice asked the question that she was beginning to get worried.

"Oh, once or twice a week."

What Beatrice didn't know was that Theresa had spent the whole weekend at Keith's place. After picking her up on Friday evening he took her to his place, and an hour later they were in bed together. Theresa was eager and very happy to enjoy everything he could offer. She was falling in love with him.

What Theresa didn't know was that Beatrice had received a phone call from Susan who told her that she had not come back to the house on the weekend, but Beatrice wasn't about to confront Theresa about this. "Remember when we talked about self-discipline?"

"Yeah." Theresa thought a lecture was coming.

"Well?"

"I'm fine; everything is good. Jimmy's not hassling me, I've met a great guy, and I've got a tutor, so my math marks are getting better. What are you worried about?"

"I'm not worried, I'm just concerned."

"Don't be, I'm happy."

“Okay.” It was hard to argue with Theresa, because what she said was true, but Beatrice knew from experience with other students that boyfriends usually meant trouble.

When the plane started its descent to the Green Star Lake airport, Jimmy looked down at his grandmother’s house. As he got out of the plane, he saw two band constables waiting to search the passengers’ bags. They gave him a big smile.

“Good to see you, Jimmy. You got any bags?”

“No, just what I got on, nowhere to hide anything unless you want to body-search me.”

“You back for a while?”

He didn’t answer. Instead he headed toward where his uncle Peter was waiting.

His uncle grabbed him by the shoulders. “It’s good to see you Jimmy, but you look like you’ve been in the bush for a year wrestling with a bear.”

“I’m okay, just tired.” Peter could see the black eyes and the bruises. It wasn’t the time to talk about it.

“Where’s my grandmother?”

“At the nursing station.”

“What’s wrong?”

“They’re not sure. She caught a cold a couple of weeks ago, but it got worse and the last couple of days it’s been pretty bad. She’s lost a lot of weight. That’s why they’re keeping her at the nursing station.”

“She’s hardly ever been sick.”

“Yes, I know, she’s always had lots of energy.” Jimmy could tell his uncle was very worried. As brother and sister, Martha and Peter had always been very close.

“I want to see her; take me to the nursing station.”

“I think I should take you home so you can get cleaned up.”

“No, I can do that later,” Jimmy’s voice was rising. “I want to go now."

Peter could see that he was about to lose his temper. "I can't stop you Jimmy, but to be honest you look like a mess, and I don't think you want your grandmother to see you right now." He spoke to him quietly then waited.

Jimmy had always had a lot of respect for his uncle, who had never deserted him no matter how difficult things had been.

"Yeah, you're right, take me home first."

When Jimmy entered the house it was cold and damp. Gone were the smells of the wood fire and his grandmother's cooking. It made Jimmy feel uncomfortable, as if somehow his home had changed.

He quickly washed and put on clean clothes, but when he saw his face in the mirror, he wondered what he would tell his grandmother.

When he entered the nursing station, he was relieved to see his favorite nurse at the front desk. She smiled at him as he approached. "Jimmy, it's good to see you."

Margaret had been at the Green Star Lake nursing station for eight years, much longer than any other nurse, many of whom found the community too chaotic. She never seemed to run out of patience and had stitched Jimmy up more than a few times. One time Jimmy had asked her if she was Cree. "Oh, mostly Cree and a little Algonquin, Jimmy."

"I want to see my grandmother."

"Yes, Jimmy, but she's sleeping right now and I don't want to wake her." She could see that Jimmy was getting agitated. She knew that he was very close to his grandmother and that Martha had been a source of strength and stability for him.

"But, I want to …" Jimmy started again.

Margaret took him by the hands. "Jimmy, just sit down, and we'll see what we can do. Okay?"

She smiled at him, but Jimmy knew that she was expecting him to listen. "I'll be back in a couple of minutes."

When she came back, she told him, "You can go sit in the room, but don't wake her up."

Jimmy nodded and followed her. When he saw his grandmother lying in bed, he was shocked. A shiver went through him when he looked at her thin, pale face.

"What's wrong, Margaret?"

"If she doesn't get better tomorrow we're going to fly her to Winnipeg."

He went over, kissed his grandmother on the cheek and sat down on a chair beside the bed. "I'll wait."

"Okay." She put her hand on his shoulder before leaving.

Jimmy tried to sleep in a chair until he heard his grandmother's voice.

"Jimmy is that you?"

He kissed her on the forehead. "Are you going to be okay?"

"We'll see. I'm so glad to see you. What happened to your face, all the scars and bruises?"

"Winnipeg's a little rough, but I'm here now so don't worry. I'm okay."

"How's Theresa?"

Jimmy didn't answer and changed the subject. "They're thinking about flying you to Winnipeg. Did you know that?"

"I trust Margaret, she wouldn't send me out unless she had to. Come here, Jimmy," and she took both her hands and put them around the back of his head and kissed his cheek. "What are you going to do now? You've missed a lot of school and you didn't answer my question about Theresa. Is she okay?"

"Yes, she's fine but not too happy with me."

"Why?"

"She's always got some reason to be disappointed with me. You know."

"Not always... You'd better go home and get some sleep. You can come back later."

Jimmy didn't want to leave. "No, I think I'll stay here for a while."

"Are you going back to school?"

Jimmy shrugged. "Don't know."

She looked at him for a long time without saying a word.

Finally, he told her, "I'll drop in and see what's going on."

"What's going on?"

"Maybe I can get back in."

She lifted her hand and put it on his chest. "You've got to want it in there, not just because I'm asking."

He knew what she meant because school was always something he did after everything else in his life.

"Yeah...okay" He didn't finish.

"You're so smart, and you could do so much if you wanted to."

"Everybody is always telling me that."

He stood beside her bed holding her frail little hand. She had put up with so much trouble from him; she had given him so much.

"You have to be strong now, just like you were when Gary took his life."

He didn't want his grandmother to see how upset he was, so he walked toward the door. "I won't let you down."

"Don't let yourself down, Jimmy," she told him. "That's the most important thing."

He went home and crawled into his own bed. It felt so good that he slept until noon the next day. Then he got up and made himself go to school.

CHAPTER 10

Theresa's Disappointment

By the middle of November, Theresa had spent many nights with Keith. Her first report card was good, although she had missed some classes and had met Bruce only once in the previous two weeks. That led to a mark of 30 per cent on her last math test.

Every time Theresa missed tutoring, Bruce found her in the hall, but Theresa could give him no good reason for being away except that she had been busy. Bruce was disappointed and told her so. "You get behind and there's no way you're going to pass, Theresa. You know that." She agreed but still didn't meet him the next time. Often she sat in class daydreaming about Keith, about the great times they spent together in bed and going out with his friends. One of the things she admired most about him was that he encouraged her to study and go to her tutoring. She understood that Keith wanted her to follow her own path, be an individual, but Theresa was starting to depend on him, to wait for his calls and look forward to the next time she would see him. She had been drawn in by his positive energy and the way he listened to her when she talked about her life. He was everything Jimmy was not. Not only was Keith one of the best-looking First Nations men she had ever known, but he was a passionate and caring lover.

Soon there were days when Theresa couldn't get out of bed because of the late nights. Susan began to knock on her door in the mornings to see if Theresa was sick. One week, she missed two days of school when she met Keith at the university. Toward the middle of November, Theresa was often sick in the morning prompting Susan to ask her about it. "Do you think it's the flu?"

"Probably," but Theresa remembered how sick she was when she was pregnant with Chance.

After three mornings in a row of listening to Theresa throw up, Susan called Beatrice. An hour later Beatrice called back.

"How are you doing?"

"Pretty good." Theresa tried to sound cheerful.

"Let's get together after school today."

"I can't today, I might be going to tutoring with Bruce."

"Might be?"

"Yeah, I think so."

"Well, I can meet you for lunch today."

Theresa was feeling pressured. "Why don't we meet on Friday at lunch?"

"Okay, I'll pick you up in front of the school."

Beatrice was worried when she got off the phone. She had seen it all too often. With the high hopes she had for Theresa, she didn't want to think about her getting pregnant.

Soon Theresa was phoning Keith most nights, hoping to find him at home. He was polite and patient with her, always listening no matter how long she wanted to talk. When she asked to go to his place, he told her she was welcome. Theresa knew that she was crowding him, phoning too often and taking too much of his time, but he continued to encourage her and to be affectionate. Even though she knew she should back off, give him more space and be more independent, she missed him when they were apart for a couple of days. She realized she was interfering with his university work, which he took seriously. Unable to stop thinking about him, she gradually felt herself drawn into behavior that embarrassed her. She feared the worst, but she had only herself to blame.

One week, Keith didn't phone at all. When Theresa didn't find him at his place, she became worried and depressed. Desperate, she took the bus to the university on Friday but couldn't find him at the student building, where he often hung out, or anywhere else on the campus.

He finally phoned on Sunday. It had been six days since she had heard from him.

She was upset. "Where have you been?"

"I went back home for a couple of days."

"But I didn't know where you were, how to get hold of you. Why not tell me what's going on? Can't you at least do that?"

"Like report in to you, Theresa?" he asked in an irritated voice.

"Okay…okay… I understand." But she didn't, and for the first time she heard a different tone in his voice, a harder sound. "When am I going to see you?" she asked.

"I'm pretty busy this week, so how about Friday?"

"That's almost a week away," she pleaded.

"I know, but I missed school last week so I have some catching up to do."

"Sure… I guess, so will I hear from you during the week?"

"I should be able to pick you up after school on Friday, but I'll phone to let you know what time. Have you been going to your tutoring and all your classes?"

"Yes," she lied, and he knew it.

Theresa wanted to shout, "I think I'm pregnant, Keith," but decided to wait until she saw him on Friday.

Theresa had missed her lunch with Beatrice on Friday and avoided her phone calls, choosing to spend much of her time in her room depressed and not eating. Susan couldn't get her to the phone when Beatrice called.

Even though Theresa didn't hear from Keith all week, she waited in front of the school until eight o'clock Friday evening. She finally took the bus home, sitting at the back where people couldn't see her sobbing. When she got home Beatrice was waiting for her.

"Hello, Theresa."

Theresa was embarrassed and unable to say anything.

Beatrice could see that she had been crying. "Let's go out for something to eat."

Theresa knew that there was no point in making excuses. She told Beatrice everything that had happened with Jimmy and Keith as well as the fact that she was pretty sure she was pregnant with Keith's baby. Besides missing tutoring for the past four weeks, she had missed most of her classes over the previous two weeks.

Beatrice listened without saying a word. Finally, she asked, "What do you see as your options?"

"I don't know."

"Does Keith know?"

"No. I've got to get a test anyway."

"Are you going to tell him if you are?"

"Don't know. I don't know when I'll see him again." She started to cry.

"Do you want to tell him?'

"Why tell him if he doesn't care about me?"

"Well, do you think he has the right to know?"

Theresa didn't answer.

Beatrice listened while Theresa talked about Keith. She could tell that Theresa was terrified that he didn't want her in his life.

"And if it's true?" Beatrice asked.

"What?"

"If he doesn't want to see you any more?"

Theresa didn't answer but broke into tears, shaking her head. "No, no…he wouldn't do that. He likes me too much. He's such a great guy, Beatrice, but I think I ruined it for us. I was so foolish."

Beatrice knew it was not the time to disagree, but to listen to Theresa and support her, to help her make a decision. Then she asked, "Are you thinking of going back home?"

"What else, if I'm pregnant? I can't stay here."

"You could if you wanted; others girls have done it."

All Theresa could think of was getting back home in case Keith phoned. "Can we go now?"

"Sure, but I want to see you in a few days."

"Yeah, okay."

After Beatrice dropped her off at home, Theresa crawled into bed and cried herself to sleep.

CHAPTER 11

Heading Home

Jimmy walked into the school office and asked to see the principal.

"We haven't seen you for a while."

"Yeah, I've been away."

"What can I do for you?"

"I'm thinking about coming back to school."

"But you missed half the term. How could you make that up?" He gave Jimmy a questioning stare.

"I will."

"You just come walking in here and figure you can start any time you please, is that it? You didn't do anything but sleep most of the time in class. Have I got that right?"

"Yeah," Jimmy grunted.

"So now you're back, you want to come to school, meet all your friends, goof around in class and sleep when you're hung over, like this is some drop-in centre."

Jimmy was getting angry but he knew it would get him nowhere if he lost his temper.

"Let me think about it; I'll let you know."

"Why can't you decide now?" Jimmy shot back.

"Because I want to think about it." Jimmy wasn't the only

one getting angry. “You’re 18 now, an adult. I want to talk to a few people. Maybe you should be taking adult upgrading.”

“When, next year?”

“I don’t know, but what I do know is that you can’t just keep drifting in and out when you feel like it.”

When the principal got up from his seat, Jimmy knew it was time to leave.

“I’ll let you know.”

But when two days had passed and he had not returned to school, his uncle asked, “Are you going to finish grade 10? You’ve just turned 18 and it’s time to finish, because you won’t want to do it later.”

“They won’t let me back in.”

“Your grandmother is really hoping you do.”

“I’ve been to see her every day; she’s better now.”

“Yes she is,” replied Peter. “Maybe your coming back helped her get better.”

When Jimmy told him about the talk he had with the principal, his uncle didn’t say a word.

That afternoon, Peter went to the school and met with the principal.

“I can understand what you’re thinking about Jimmy, but I know him. If he gives you his word that he’s going to do something, he’ll do it. I can vouch for him, besides, he’s not going to let his grandmother down again. I know that for sure. Just ask him what he’s prepared to do.”

And then Peter left.

The principal had already decided to keep Jimmy out of school, but he knew better than to ignore the visit from Peter. Peter now, but maybe a band counsellor next. He’d wait Jimmy out. Having read Jimmy’s file, the principal knew that he was bad news, and it was only a matter of time before Jimmy would find a way to get himself put out again. He’d never last more than a week or two before there was trouble.

He was back in school the next morning.

"What are you planning on doing this time around?" the principal asked.

"I'll get the highest marks in the class," Jimmy said, challenging the principal with a stare.

It was a short discussion. "I hope I won't be seeing you back in my office."

"Don't hold your breath," Jimmy replied and stormed out of the office to his first class.

As he walked down the hall, Theresa's last words rang in his brain:"You're a loser."

Nobody calls me that, he thought as he opened the door to his grade 10 history class.

When Beatrice phoned Theresa at noon on Sunday, Susan answered.

"She's still sleeping; do you want me to get her up?"

"No, just tell her I'll pick her up at 6."

That evening Beatrice and Theresa went for coffee, but Theresa had little to say as she sat in the booth staring off into space.

"You don't look well," Beatrice told her.

"Haven't been sleeping too well, got a few things on my mind."

"So why don't you tell me what you're thinking." When she didn't answer, Beatrice gave her a big hug.

"You're going to get through this because I know you're strong enough. Let's figure out what we can do. First of all I've made an appointment for you with a doctor close to where you live."

"I know I am, I bought one of those pregnancy kits from the drugstore."

"Did you go to school this week?"

"A couple of times."

Beatrice had been to the school to talk to Janet, Theresa's school counsellor.

"Maybe she's been here once or twice in the last two weeks," Janet said. "I sat down with her, but she was completely different, wouldn't say a word. She was doing so well, she was happy, working, making good progress with her tutor, and then just a complete collapse. It's hard to believe. What's going on?"

"Man problems." That's all Beatrice would tell Janet for the time being. It was not the time to tell her Theresa was pregnant until she had a better idea what Theresa was going to do.

In the coffee shop, Beatrice sat beside Theresa holding her hand. "Why don't you think about trying to stay in school, at least until Christmas? You had such a good start, one of my best students. Is there any way I can help you make it through this while you're here in Winnipeg?"

She tried to get Theresa to talk but ended up doing most of the talking, encouraging her, but Theresa's mind was not at the restaurant. All she could think about was Keith. She'd been to his place several times, but either he was out or he refused to answer the door when he realized who it was.

"You're waiting for him, aren't you?"

Theresa nodded and started crying. "We were so happy, so good together."

Beatrice put her arm around her. "I know it's tough not hearing from him, but do you think it's a good idea to keep hoping he'll come back?

"I know, but I can't live without him, I just can't."

They were the words that Beatrice feared the most— "can't live without him". The thought of suicide flashed through her mind. She had lost a friend that way six years ago, and the memory still haunted her.

“I know that you’re not going to believe this, but some day in the future you’ll get over him. I know that’s hard to believe.”

“No, that’s not going to happen.” Theresa got up and walked toward the door.

On the way home, Beatrice decided it was time to get more realistic. “You’ve got your son at home and another baby on the way, so what about them? Do you think they’re more important than you or Keith right now? This is not just about what you want, Theresa.”

Theresa turned and stared at her, thinking that Beatrice had no right to judge her, but when she thought of Chance and the new life inside her, it made her realize for the first time how little she had thought about her son lately. She felt guilty. “Okay, you’re right, maybe I’m being selfish, but I love Keith. I’m sorry I can’t be stronger; I wish I could.”

“You are strong enough. You just have to decide what’s best for all of you right now.”

As she got out of the car, she told Beatrice, “I’ll call you in two days, I promise.”

Two days later, Theresa went to Nick’s house, hoping she could find Keith. A couple of guys were hanging around the house.

“Hey, look who came back for more fun.”

She tried to remain calm. “Have you seen Keith?” They laughed at her.

“Are you going to tell me?”

“We don’t need to tell you shit, but maybe if you want to come into the house with me I could make you happy. You tell that asshole Jimmy that if we ever get our hands on him he’ll never walk again.”

Theresa stood glued to the sidewalk, staring at them, knowing she was humiliating herself.

They sneered at her. “Keith’s through with you. He had his fun.”

“You don’t know that.”

They began to laugh louder and told her to leave. Right then, Theresa decided that it was time to go back home to Green Star Lake.

CHAPTER 12

A Surprise Visitor

Bruce looked out the window as the plane circled above the community. Green Star Lake was so small he wondered how people were doing. The plane hit the gravel runway, and soon he was on the landing strip facing two band policemen.

"Open up your bags." Bruce looked at all the luggage from the plane spread out on the ground.

"What are you looking for?" Bruce asked as he opened his bags. "Are you looking for drugs?"

The band constable made a quick check and just smiled. "You can go now."

When Bruce walked into the small terminal he was surrounded by a crowd of people. Some had just flown in and some were flying out. Kids were running around the room and babies were crying. He approached a young man. "Can you tell me where Theresa lives?"

He stopped and eyed Bruce up and down then shouted to his friends, "Hey Dave, here's the guy who knocked up Theresa."

"What…what are you talking about?" Bruce stammered. "I didn't knock anybody up."

"Then what are you doing up here, asshole?"

They all laughed, and one yelled, "He came to Green Star

for a holiday!"

"No."

They crowded around asking him questions. "I'm a friend, I used to help her with her math."

"You didn't do a very good job if she had to come back."

An older man stepped forward. "I'll take you to her house. Come on."

As he left another one yelled, "Bye daddy, I hope you brought lots of money, white boy."

The picture of his meeting Theresa in Janet's office for the first time popped up in his head. Had his first reaction to her been any different from the way those guys had treated him? Being out of his comfortable surroundings made him feel nervous.

"Just ignore them. My name is Curtis. You planning on staying long in Green Star?"

"I don't know how long, Curtis."

Bruce was surprised when he saw some rundown houses and a few places destroyed by fire, but he also saw houses that looked neat and well taken care of. He looked at all the trucks, some new, a few old and rusted.

Curtis pulled up in front of a small, well-kept house.

When Theresa's mother saw Bruce, her first thought was that this was the boy who had made her daughter pregnant. When Bruce saw the frosty reception, he quickly introduced himself. "Hi, I'm Bruce, a friend of Theresa's from school."

Theresa's mother relaxed because she knew that the father's name was Keith. "She's over at a friend's house."

Bruce stood at the door, wondering what he should do next. She invited him in and offered him tea and biscuits. It was awkward until he explained about tutoring Theresa in math.

"Oh yes, Theresa told me about you."

When Theresa came through the door she stopped and

stared him, then shouted, “Bruce, what are you doing here?”

She gave him a big hug. “I’m shocked; you in Green Star Lake!”

“Is that so different? Theresa in Winnipeg?”

“But what are you doing here?”

“They wouldn’t tell me anything about why you left, so I came to find out for myself. I just learned at the airport here that you’re going to have a baby. That explains everything.”

She was surprised that she was so happy to see him. “I see some books sticking out of those bags. Oh, oh, I think I know why you’re up here, Bruce.”

“Yeah Theresa, but that’s not the only reason I came. I wanted to get away from home, come up here, see where you live. When I got up a couple of days ago on my eighteenth birthday, I decided it was time to quit hanging around home and my parents.”

“How long are you planning on staying?”

“A couple of weeks, maybe.”

“What about school?”

“I can pass without the last two or three weeks before Christmas.”

“Two weeks,” Theresa blurted out. She began to wonder where he’d stay and whether her mother would let him sleep on the couch.

“You came a long way to figure out I was pregnant.”

“I had to; they wouldn’t tell me anything at the school. Is there a place I can stay, a motel or a hotel?”

Theresa and her mom began to laugh. “The closest hotel is 200 miles away.”

“Can I pay someone to put me up?”

“You can stay here until you decide what you’re going to do.”

They sat at the kitchen table talking for a couple of hours while her mom sat and listened. Finally she said, “You brought books, why?"

"Why not?"

Theresa laughed, "You don't give up do you?"

"Should I?"

"So have you got a girlfriend now?" she joked with him.

"Not a girlfriend but girls interested in me. I have to say you were right when you said relax, shut up and listen."

"That's great, Bruce, but it's no reason to come up here and save me."

"It's not just that Theresa it's...well...I'm hoping that you'll come back to school."

Theresa took his hand. "Bruce, that's so nice but I can't ...."

He stopped her. "You're smart, you can do it, and I can help you. Believe me."

"This is so crazy...just crazy... a white boy up in the north with books and no place to stay."

"That's not important right now, but after listening to you talk about the north and your home I wanted to experience it. I know it sounds weird, but it was something I knew I had to do."

Theresa was speechless, but her mother said, "You're a good boy, but what do your mother and father think?"

"To tell you truth, we had a big fight when I told them I wanted to come up here for a few weeks to visit you. When they told me I couldn't go, something just snapped in my head. I told them I wasn't their little boy any more, willing to agree with everything they wanted. Right there, at that moment, that life was over for me. It was so sudden. It wasn't their choice any more. When my mom and dad dropped me off at the airport, they were very worried that something would happen to me, you know, get into drinking and drugs or get beat up or worse, but I told them I didn't want them protecting me any more. Do you understand Theresa, I just turned eighteen, it was time to experience life on my own. I knew it was something I had to do. Right now, this is more important than school. They can't understand that right now, but they will."

"But why didn't you wait until the summer?"

"Because I might never have done it if I hadn't just made up my mind right then and got on that plane. The decision to do it might have just faded away."

"But what are you going to do here?"

"I've brought all the assignments and tests you've missed."

Theresa smiled at him. "You're really nuts, Bruce...you know we never should have had that talk that night. Look what's happened to you."

Her mother interrupted. "Would you like a big piece of pie, Bruce?"

Bruce slept on the couch for three days. During the day he worked with Theresa, who was reluctant at first but finally give in to his nonstop enthusiasm.

At supper on the third day, her mom made a suggestion. "There's an Elder about a half mile up the lake, living by himself. Lucas is getting old, but he wants to stay up there even though it's getting hard for him to live on his own at his cabin. He could use someone to help him, Bruce."

"Does he have a place for me to sleep?" He tried to imagine what it would be like living in a cabin in the bush with a frail old man.

"Yes, he's got a fairly big place he and his kids built many years ago. The roof needs some repairs, but I should also tell you he's one of the best hunters and fishermen in the community."

"How do I get back and forth?"

"His snowmobile, when it's working, otherwise you walk."

The last school week before Christmas, Bruce started working in the school, helping the little kids with their work. In the morning he was at the school, and in the afternoons he worked with Theresa.

Jimmy saw Bruce working in the classroom and remembered him from Theresa's school in the city. When Jimmy heard he was living with Lucas in the bush he wondered what the strange white guy would do next.

Bruce came to the community almost every day, except when he was working around the cabin or when the two of them were hunting, something that required Bruce to use a rifle, a totally new and somewhat frightening experience. Living with Lucas required a radical change in his diet. He had never lived on five or six basic foods—fish, moose meat, potatoes, bannock, a few vegetables and caribou. They were the main dishes. Most nights he went to bed exhausted from trekking through the snow and the other physical demands of his new life. In the morning when the cabin was cold, he asked himself why he was doing this, but he always started the day with enthusiasm and determination. He had talked to his parents once who demanded that he come home. They even threatened to contact the RCMP, but he reminded them he was 18, and it was pointless for them to make idle threats. He loved his parents; they had always been good to him, but he knew that his decision to break away from them had been the right one. They were going to have to accept it and realize that the relationship had been profoundly changed.

Lucas didn't speak much, and his English wasn't very good, but Bruce listened and slowly began to understand his pronunciation. He noticed how Lucas came alive when he spoke Cree to people in the community, and that encouraged Bruce to try learning it. Lucas got a big kick out of his Cree pronunciation but didn't tire of trying to get him to speak his language.

Theresa saw him almost every day. She began to notice small changes in his attitude. An easy-going, assertive confidence began to appear although he often smelled like a man who had been in the bush for too long, unshaven and dirty. When she looked at him, she wished she could be interested in him romantically, but knew that they would only be friends. It had been decided that night in the car.

She continued to try to understand why he was in Green Star Lake. Was he trying to prove something to her or to himself? Did he still want to be her partner or think he was doing it as a way of thanking her for the radical change in his life? Could she really have had that much influence over him?

One of the most difficult things for Theresa was having to speak to his parents, who desperately wanted to get information about him. She told them he was doing well for a white man in the bush. She knew this didn't make them happy. Bruce told her he had made a mistake in giving them her phone number.

Bruce and Lucas spent Christmas at Theresa's home. Bruce supplied all the food. He told her mother, "You've often been feeding me since I've been here; I figure it's time I finally did my share."

Jimmy dropped over with a present for Chance. Theresa's mother invited him in, but he wouldn't go beyond a couple of feet past the front door.

"I've got to get going."

Jimmy picked his son up and kissed him when Chance ran over and grabbed his leg.

Just before Jimmy left, Bruce got up and shook his hand. "Merry Christmas."

"Yeah," Jimmy grunted quietly. Then he was gone.

"That was a surprise, Mom."

"Yes, it was."

After dinner they talked at the kitchen table. "Are you going back next week?"

"I don't think so. I talked to the principal here, and he'll supervise my exams if the school will send them up."

"What do you mean? How long are you going to stay?"

"Not sure, but I'm learning more from Lucas and being in Green Star Lake than I'd get at school. I'll know when it's time to leave. Spring must be pretty nice up here."

There was a long silence between the two of them and Bruce knew what she was thinking. "You afraid to go back?" he asked.

"Maybe, afraid I'd run into Keith, afraid I'd fail at school, afraid I'd get into trouble, lots of afraids, Bruce."

"What about your counsellor?"

"I've talked to her several times since I came back. She wants me to come back to school even though I'm having the baby in the middle of July."

"Look, we're caught up with the work; just go back and write a few tests. Your teachers will let you do it. Get Janet to talk to them."

Her mother was listening to the conversation, "Why not, Theresa? I don't like to see you go, but I can look after Chance. I know in your heart it's what you really want to do."

"What?"

"Finish high school."

Theresa knew it was true. She felt stronger and more confident. Before her mother went to bed, she asked Theresa, "Did Beatrice find him?"

Theresa looked at the pained expression on her mom's face, "Not yet, Mom, but she hasn't given up."

She wished she could have told her that her dad was coming home because Theresa knew how much her mom missed him. It was one of the reasons Theresa wanted to go back to Winnipeg. Finding him meant everything to her.

On January 5, the plane was on the runway waiting to take on passengers. Bruce and Theresa's mother were standing with her and Chance. Bruce hugged her for a long time.

"I'll phone you, Theresa."

She had tears in her eyes when she looked at her mother. "Don't worry this time, Mom. The next time I get off that plane I'll be in grade 12."

"I know. I believe you."

As she was walking toward the plane, she yelled to her mother, "And I'll have another baby for you to look after."

When she reached the stairs to the plane, she saw Jimmy standing behind the fence, looking at her. She stopped and stared at him. He slowly raised his arm with the thumbs-up sign.

As Bruce passed Jimmy on the way out of the airport, Jimmy called out to him, "I'm watching you."

"Yeah, I figured," Bruce called back.

www.ingramcontent.com/pod-product-compliance
Lightning Source LLC
LaVergne TN
LVHW020654100826
845148LV00012B/2479